The Ma

The Mystery of the Cursed Elves

By Mitchel Maree
Illustrations by Ola Snimshchikova

This is a work of fiction. Names, characters, places, and incidents either are the product of the author's imagination or are used fictitiously. Any resemblance to actual persons, living or dead, events, or locales is entirely coincidental.

First paperback edition October 2020
Second paperback edition April 2021

ISBN 978-1-7360656-0-0: (paperback)

www.mitchelmaree.com

For my children:
Maddex, Mila, Khaleesi, and Roxi

Contents

Chapter One

The Visitor in the Shed

Max Watson woke up to the sun streaming through his window. He jumped out of bed and threw back the curtains. After a week-long rainy spell, he couldn't wait to get outside. He quickly got dressed before bursting out of his room.

"The sun's out," he yelled, thundering

through the hall and down the stairs.

"What's all that noise?" his father asked when Max came barreling into the kitchen.

"The sun's out," Max repeated, gesturing toward the window. "I need to get out."

Grabbing his sweatshirt and shoes, Max was out the door.

Max was the oldest of four children and the only boy. Though lonely at times, his active imagination and love for adventure kept him entertained.

Back inside the house, the three Watson girls made their way slowly down the stairs.

"Max woke us up," Sophie whined to her father.

"He's outside already," Dad commented.

Sophie rolled her eyes dramatically. As the oldest girl, she felt it was her responsibility to look after her siblings and keep them safe.

Violet was the perfect example of a typical middle child. She was quiet, observant, and easily followed along with her more dominant siblings. Like Max, she had a highly active imagination, but *she believed* in all things magical.

Parker, the youngest, was absolutely fearless. She threw caution to the wind, running into things headfirst without a second thought.

"Let's go see what Max is doing," Parker said, not wanting to miss out on anything.

"I'm still sleepy," Sophie whined.

"I'm hungry," Violet added.

"Suit yourself; I'm going out," Parker said.

"Why don't you all go outside?" Mom suggested. "I'll make pancakes and call you when they're ready."

"Fine." Sophie gave another eye roll.

"Get your scooters," Max called when the girls came out. "Let's race down the street."

Sophie walked to the shed and scrunched her nose at the mess. Dad had shoved things haphazardly into the shed last week in a rush to get everything under cover before the rain came. Sophie spotted her scooter buried underneath some patio chairs. Violet peered around her sister, looking for her own scooter.

"Sophie, look back there," Violet said.

"What? Where?" Sophie struggled to pull the tangled chairs off her scooter.

"In the corner, what is that?" Violet said.

"It looks like a stuffed toy," Sophie told her. "Dad probably tossed it in last week.

Parker, did you leave one of your dolls outside?"

"What?" Parker brought her scooter to a skidding stop in front of the shed.

"There's a doll in the back of the shed," Sophie pointed.

"I'll get it." Parker climbed over the pile of patio furniture. She retrieved the toy and brought it out. "It's an elf doll."

Parker set the elf on the ground, moving back so everyone could see.

"Whose elf is it?" Violet asked, leaning down to examine the doll. "Wait, what is it holding?"

The elf was holding a cube in its hands.

"How is that cube staying there?" Sophie asked.

Max shrugged, reaching down and taking

the cube from the elf's hands.

"This looks like one of those fidget cubes," he said, pushing and pressing the various buttons and switches.

Suddenly, there was a burst of light, followed by complete darkness. Seconds later, the sun was shining again.

"Wh...what just happened?" Violet's eyes widened as she looked around.

"Where's the elf?" Parker pointed to where the elf had just been sitting.

The elf was gone.

"Max took it," Sophie accused, not amused.

"No, I didn't," Max shook his head, holding out his empty hands as proof.

"It's over there." Violet pointed toward the shed.

The kids turned toward the shed. The elf was *standing* in the doorway.

"How is it just standing there?" Max questioned.

The elf waved at the children. Once he had their attention, he turned and disappeared into the shed.

"I think he wants us to follow him," Violet said.

"I'm not going in there," Sophie put her hands up in protest.

"Step aside," Parker rushed into the shed.

"Parker, get back here," Sophie said firmly. "You are not going in there."

"Too late," Violet muttered.

"Parker, get out here," Sophie called, peeking into the shed. "Parker? I don't see her."

"What? We all watched her go in." Max rolled his eyes as he walked into the shed after Parker.

"Do you see her, Max?" Sophie called out. Max did not reply. "Now, *he's* not answering."

Violet stepped toward the shed. Sophie grabbed Violet's arm to stop her.

"No way are we going in there," Sophie told her.

"It's just a shed, Sophie," Violet pulled her arm free and stepped into the shed.

"You guys, come back," Sophie demanded. "I'll get Mom and Dad."

No one responded.

Sophie poked her head into the shed. "Max? Violet? Parker?"

With a huff of impatience, Sophie tiptoed

carefully into the shed. It wasn't a large shed. She could easily make out the back wall; however, her siblings were gone.

"This isn't funny, guys."

Sophie tripped and stumbled her way to the back of the shed. As she neared the wall, her ankle became twisted in a hose, and she fell forward. Expecting to hit the wall, Sophie was shocked when she landed with a gentle thud in something soft, cold, and wet.

"Snow?" Sophie looked down at the white powder around her.

Standing up, she brushed herself off and was startled by the thick jacket she now wore. The light sweatshirt she had put on this morning was now a large puffy jacket. Her jeans had been replaced by snow pants, and thick winter boots now covered her feet.

She felt things bulging in her coat pockets. Reaching in one side, she pulled out a pair of thick gloves, and in the other pocket, she found a wool hat. Quickly, she put both on as the cold surrounded her.

"We are definitely not in the backyard anymore."

Chapter Two

The House in the Woods

"Think fast," Max yelled, tossing a snowball toward his sisters.

"This is so amazing," Violet screamed with excitement rolling up a snowball of her own.

"Where are we?" Sophie asked. "What is this place?"

Sophie turned around, hoping to see the shed, but all that was behind her was an endless row of snow-covered trees.

"Where did the shed go?" Sophie asked nervously.

"I don't know where we are, but look at all the snow," Parker said, flopping down and making a snow angel.

Suddenly, the elf appeared at the top of the hill. He made several gestures before jumping down onto his belly and sliding down the hill.

Parker ran after the elf, watching in amazement as he slid all the way to the bottom of the steep hill. The elf stood up and waved at her, motioned them all to follow.

"We better get down there," Parker told them.

"I'm not sliding on my belly all the way down there," Sophie said firmly.

"We don't have to, look," Max spotted two sleds propped against a tree. "We can take those down."

"No way," Sophie said, shaking her head.

"Come on, Sophie, don't be such a chicken," Parker teased. "You can ride with me."

Max walked over and grabbed the two sleds. He handed one to Parker and placed the other on the ground in front of him.

"Get in front, Violet, let's do this," Max said.

Violet sat down, grasping onto the sides of the sled tightly. Max sat behind her and kicked off with his foot.

"Here. We. Gooooooo," Max yelled.

Violet let out a scream as they raced down the hill. Max laughed as the snow blasted all around him.

The sled hit the bottom of the hill and skidded to a stop. Max turned around and motioned up to the girls still at the top.

"All aboard," Parker said as she hopped onto the second sled.

"No way," Sophie crossed her arms in defiance, "That looks dangerous."

"Just hold on to me and keep your eyes closed. We'll be at the bottom before you know it," Parker told her. "Unless you want to stay up here all alone."

Sophie grumbled. Reluctantly, and with much huffing and puffing, she sat down on the back of the sled, grabbing Parker tightly around the waist.

"Hold on," Parker yelled.

"I am," Sophie said sharply.

Parker pushed off with her foot, and the sled shot forward. Sophie screamed as they raced down the hill at what felt like light speed.

"Slow down, slow down," Sophie yelled.

"I don't think we can," Parker yelled back, laughing. "Isn't this fun?"

"No," Sophie replied, squeezing her eyes shut.

"I don't know how to stop this thing,"

Parker yelled as they came rushing toward the bottom of the hill. "Lean to the right."

Sophie kept her eyes closed as Parker leaned them toward the right. The whole sled flipped over, sending Parker and Sophie sprawling into the soft snow.

"That was amazing," Parker said, jumping up and wiping off her pants.

Sophie rolled her eyes at her younger sister as she sat up, trying to catch her breath.

"That was so fun," Max said.

"I could do that all day," Parker agreed.

"There's the elf," Violet pointed toward the trees.

"Follow him," Max said.

"Should we be blindly following a toy elf into these creepy woods?" Sophie asked suspiciously.

"We've come this far," Max replied. "We might as well see where he's taking us."

They broke out of the trees and stood in front of a huge house. The house looked just like the gingerbread house they had made last Christmas. The windows seemed to be outlined in red licorice, and two large candy cane poles stood on either side of a door that resembled a chocolate bar. The snow on the roof looked just like Mom's homemade frosting.

"Am I the only one who is suddenly very hungry?" Parker licked her lips.

The children climbed the steps to stand next to the elf at the front door. Violet noticed the elf was no longer a tiny doll but stood at the same height as her.

The elf gave three quick raps on the door before it was opened by another elf.

This elf was dressed in the same red and white striped shirt as the first elf but wore a red skirt instead of pants. A purple hat covered her two braids.

"It's about time you got back," she said to the first elf. "We expected you a half-hour ago."

"Sorry, it took them a lot longer to find me than I expected," the first elf said.

"Hi, I'm Winnie," the elf inside the house said, addressing the children. "This is Scout."

Scout gave a little wave as the children stood staring, their mouths open in amazement.

"Please come in," Winnie stepped back.

The children followed Winnie down a

hallway and into a large open room. A table ran the length of the room with chairs and benches skillfully placed down each side.

"Look at this table," Parker said. "It's so long."

"We need room for all the elves," Winnie replied.

"There are more of you?" Sophie asked in disbelief.

"Of course," Winnie said. "This *is* the North Pole, after all."

"The North Pole?" Violet's eyes widened. "If this is the North Pole, then that means..."

"Ho ho ho. Hello, children," a booming voice finished her thought.

"Santa," Violet gasped.

"Santa?" Max repeated in disbelief.

Turning toward the doorway, Max stared

at the man standing there. Sure enough, he was an older man, wearing red, with a full white beard and a large belly.

"I have no idea what's happening," Sophie mumbled to herself. "I'm dreaming. I have to be dreaming."

Parker reached over and pinched her oldest sister's arm.

"Ow, what was that for?" Sophie asked sharply.

"It's not a dream," Parker winked.

"I'm so glad you're here," Santa said. "The elves need your help. It seems some of the elves have, well, there's no easy way to put this; the elves have gone bad."

Chapter Three

Cookies with Santa

"The elves have gone bad?" Violet repeated.

"Oh, the children are here," a soft voice interrupted their conversation.

"Mrs. Claus," Violet whispered in awe.

Mrs. Claus stood behind them, her hands clasped in front of her, and a full, welcoming smile spread across her face.

"Come, sit down, let me get you some cookies and cocoa," Mrs. Claus motioned toward the table. "Everyone get settled, then we can talk."

Mrs. Claus headed out of the room.

"I love cookies," Parker hurried over to sit down first.

While the children got settled, removing their hats and gloves, Mrs. Claus returned with a plate of fresh cookies. Behind her, Winnie carried a tray of steaming hot cocoa. Each child took a cookie and a mug of cocoa.

"Marshmallows," Sophie commented, peering into her mug.

"These are so good," Parker said, her mouth full of cookie.

Winnie sat down at the end of the table. Santa and Mrs. Claus sat across from the children.

"I know you have questions," Winnie stated as the children ate.

"Is our shed magic?" Sophie asked.

"No," Winnie told her. "The cube you found is what opens the portal."

"The portal?" Violet's jaw fell open.

"The portal that brought you here to help us," Winnie said.

"What did you mean the elves have gone bad?" Max questioned.

"Most of them have gone bad," Winnie pointed out. "There are still a few of us who aren't affected."

"What do you mean by bad?" Sophie asked.

"Bad, evil, mean," Winnie explained. "These elves destroy things, like the toys, and they leave a trail of destruction behind.

At first, only a few elves were acting up. Now, elves are disappearing left and right, only to reappear to cause mischief and mayhem. We don't know what is causing them to change."

"It started about a week ago," Mrs. Claus told them. "The Workshop was filled with bad elves. They were destroying all the toys and tormenting the working elves."

"We'll never be ready in time for Christmas if the bad elves keep damaging everything," Santa said.

"No Christmas," Violet wailed.

"How can we help?" Sophie asked.

"Please say I can drive the sleigh," Parker begged.

"Can we make toys?" Violet asked, thrilled at the thought.

Santa laughed his deep laugh.

"I love how enthusiastic you all are," he commented. "Sorry to let you down, but the elves are more important to me than Christmas. We need you to help us find them and return them to normal. First, we save the elves, *then* we save Christmas."

"How can we save the elves?" Max said. "We're just a bunch of kids."

"Being a kid doesn't matter," Santa told them. "Children have the best imaginations. I believe you four will succeed in saving the elves and Christmas."

"How do you know which elves are naughty and which are nice?" Violet asked.

"Their clothes lose all color and turn gray," Winnie told her. "Any elf not wearing a red striped shirt and colorful hat has been changed."

"We can help you," Parker said confidently.

"That's the spirit," Santa said with a clap. "Winnie, show them the Workshop. I have a list to go through."

"Don't forget to check it twice," Violet joked.

Santa gave a wink as he and Mrs. Claus left the room. The children stared at one another in disbelief.

"I don't know about this…uh, mission," Max told them. "How are we supposed to save the elves? Where do we even start?"

"This is all a bit strange," Sophie agreed with her brother. "Maybe we should just go home."

"What about Christmas?" Violet asked

boldly. "What about the elves? They *chose* us to help them. We can't abandon them."

Max and Sophie turned to stare at Violet, who rarely spoke her mind.

"I agree with Violet," Parker chimed in. "Scout picked us for a reason. Besides, doesn't this sound like an exciting adventure?"

"You two can stay here or go home," Violet said firmly, shoving a hand back into her glove. "I'm going with Winnie."

"Me too," Parker reached for her own gloves.

"Okay, if it's that important to you," Max said. "Maybe we can help."

The siblings slipped back into their gloves and hats before following Winnie through the back door. Behind the house stood two large buildings. The massive building directly in front of them was the Workshop. The second building, to the right, was a classic red barn with a large fence that circled half the yard.

"Is that where the reindeer live?" Violet asked, pointing toward the barn.

"Yes," Winnie told them. "We'll meet them next, but first, I'll show you the Workshop."

They all walked up to the larger building and waited in anticipation as Winnie pulled open the door. The children gasped in both delight and alarm as they followed Winnie into the building. The inside was much larger than it appeared from the outside. However, it was a disaster; stuff was strewn everywhere.

"Looks like your room," Max said to Sophie with a laugh.

Sophie glared at her brother.

"Welcome to the Workshop," Winnie said.

Chapter Four

Cursed Elves

"It doesn't normally look like this," Winnie said with a nervous laugh. "This is the work of the bad elves."

The Workshop was huge, extending back so far that it was difficult to make out the rear wall. Along both side walls, tables laid in rows covered with various tools, parts, pieces, and what looked like toys in the process of being built. Paint spilled over one

table and dripped onto the ground in a giant purple puddle.

The entire room looked as if someone had dumped a truckload of random toys through the ceiling, leaving a chaotic mess of brightly colored bits and pieces scattered over the entire floor.

"These long tables are for assembling all the toys," Winnie explained, leading them further into the Workshop.

They weaved through heads of dolls, plush toy stuffing, broken crayons, cracked tea sets, and train tracks mangled and bent as they made their way toward the middle of the Workshop.

Balls were sliced and deflated, bikes sat with tires slashed, and skateboards had been split in two. It was overwhelming to see so many toys lying in pieces.

Standing between two staircases which led to a second floor, was a conveyor belt that had seen better days. The conveyor belt was littered with broken pieces of metal and plastic. The front panel was torn off the machine, and wires hung loosely from within. A screwdriver had been shoved into the side.

"When this conveyor belt is working, we use it to send the completed toys upstairs for inspection and testing," Winnie explained.

"I can't believe those elves caused all this damage," Sophie said quietly.

"It's hard for me to understand, too," Winnie told them, tears glistening in her eyes. "Behind this staircase is where we make all the books. We call it the library."

The area behind the staircase was lined with bookshelves. Most rows were neat and tidy; however, one row of shelves had crashed down, toppled on top of one another like a row of dominos.

Books lay scattered, covering the floor. Some books were torn open, pages ripped out and thrown around the room.

A noise came from somewhere along the back wall.

"What was that?" Sophie whispered.

"It's coming from over there," Winnie kept her voice low as she motioned for them to follow her.

Tiptoeing as quietly as one can through piles of crinkling paper, they made their way slowly toward the source of the noise. As they neared the back of the Workshop, they came upon a stack of books. The top of a pink hat could be seen just over the top of the book wall.

"Sammie?" Winnie questioned. "What are you doing back here?"

"Hiding," Sammie answered in a whisper. She popped her head over the books, her eyes darting around wildly.

"Hiding from what?" Winnie asked.

"Those grey elves," Sammie said, her eyes still scanning the room. "They came in while I was out front trying to clean up the mess. They laughed at me and started breaking more things. I tried to stop them, they shoved me out of the way and began throwing things at me. I ran back here and made a fortress to hide behind."

"How long have you been hiding here?" Winnie asked.

Sammie shrugged, "Not that long. I thought they found me, but it turned out to be you, I heard."

Winnie's eyes immediately darted around the room. Max felt a chill run down his spine.

"Is there another way out?" he questioned.

Winnie shook her head.

The elves were still in here.

Sammie started sobbing loudly. Winnie reached out toward her friend. Before Winnie could touch her, Sammie's sobs turned to laughter. Winnie let her outstretched hand drop as she stared at Sammie in confusion.

Sammie laughed louder, pushing against the stack in front of her causing the books to topple over. Winnie took a step back as Sammie stood up, still laughing.

Suddenly, Sammie's shirt began flashing as if someone were turning a light on and off. The shirt flashed different colors, turning from red and white to green and purple before slowly fading to a dull grey. Sammie's pants and shoes also turned grey. Finally, her hat dimmed as all color left her outfit, and she stood entirely in grey.

Sammie lifted her head to look at Winnie, her gaze creepy, lacking all emotion.

"Death to Christmas," Sammie said in a robotic voice, followed by a mechanical laugh.

Without warning, Sammie reached down, grabbed a book, and threw it directly toward Winnie. Winnie managed to duck just in time. The book flew over her head and straight past Max's ear.

Out of nowhere, several elves, all clad in grey clothing, appeared on top of the still-standing shelves.

Sammie reached out for Winnie, but Max managed to grab her and pull her back toward him.

"Join us," one elf said in the same robotic tone Sammie had spoken. *"End Christmas forever."*

"We need to get out of here," Max whispered urgently, taking a step back while trying to keep both Sammie, and the elves overhead, in his sights.

Quickly, Winnie and the children ran down the aisle. Books flew in their direction, landing mere inches behind them. They could hear the elves laughing as they ran.

"Keep going!" Max called.

Just as Sophie rounded the staircase, the sound of breaking glass echoed from behind them. Turning, Max saw the elves jumping through a window at the back of the room.

"I think they're gone," Max said.

"Did they just go out the window?" Sophie asked.

Winnie shrugged, too emotional to speak. Tears began to well in her eyes, but she refused to let them fall.

"Winnie? Are you in here?" someone called from the front of the Workshop.

"It could be a trap," Max warned.

"I can see a blue hat," Parker said, standing on the stairs. "We're good."

"Hayden," Winnie called. "We're over

here."

"Oh, Winnie," Hayden said out of breath. "It's Dancer. He's missing!"

Chapter Five

A Missing Reindeer

"This is Hayden," Winnie told the children. "He looks after the reindeer."

After quick introductions, she turned back to Hayden, "What do you mean, Dancer is missing?"

"I was cleaning up from lunch," Hayden began. "I was in the barn; all the reindeer had gone out to the yard. When I went outside to refill the water, I noticed Dancer was missing. I thought maybe he went back inside. When I looked in his stall, he wasn't there. I looked all over the yard. He's gone."

"What do the other reindeer say about it?" Winnie asked.

"They don't know," Hayden told her, throwing his hands in the air. "You know how reindeer are. They don't notice anything, especially when they're playing their reindeer games."

"Let's go take a look." Winnie led the way out of the Workshop and toward the barn.

They counted seven reindeer in the fenced yard. Two reindeer were jumping and leaping, two more were doing flips in the air, and the rest were chasing one another around the pen.

"That's cool," Max commented. "I didn't

know they could flip like that."

"They can fly, you know," Violet reminded him.

"Only on Christmas Eve," Hayden said. "The rest of the time, they're grounded. Could you imagine if they flew around all year?"

Hayden and Winnie laughed at the thought. Violet looked shyly away, feeling a little embarrassed.

"Oh, we aren't laughing at you," Hayden placed a reassuring hand on Violet's shoulder. "It's just, the reindeer can be like little kids—no offense—they have a mind of their own. If they flew all year, we'd never be able to keep them in one place."

"They have a sparkle to them," Parker liked the way the light caused their fur to

glisten and shine.

"Magical reindeer," Hayden commented. "That's how we can tell which ones have magic and which ones are just regular reindeer."

"You're right; I don't see Dancer anywhere," Winnie said, looking over each reindeer carefully.

"Do you think the bad elves took him?" There was a hint of fear in Hayden's voice.

Suddenly, a loud crash echoed through the yard.

"What was that?" Winnie asked, looking around.

"It's coming from the shed," Hayden pointed behind the barn.

"The sleigh!" Winnie and Hayden shouted at once.

They all dashed toward the small shed behind the barn. The door was wide open. Inside, the sleigh was covered with grey elves, who were banging the sides with hammers, leaving large dents.

"Hey, stop that," Winnie yelled, standing just outside the door.

The elves stopped, turning in robotic unison to face Winnie and Hayden.

"This is creepy," Sophie said through clenched teeth.

After what seemed like an eternity, one of the grey elves spoke, *"End Christmas. Destroy Christmas."*

Soon all the elves joined in chanting, *"End Christmas. End Christmas."*

They were standing in a line, chanting while stomping their feet in rhythm.

"Where is Dancer?" Hayden yelled.

The elves turned their heads toward Hayden. Then, they marched forward.

"This isn't good," Violet said under her breath.

"Back up, back up!" Max yelled.

"I'm not afraid of you," Hayden shouted at the elves, standing his ground. "Where is Dancer?"

"Hayden," Winnie warned, reaching out for him. "Don't let them touch you."

"Hayden, move!" Max yelled, seconds too late.

The elves reached out and grabbed Hayden. They pulled him to the ground and surrounded him.

"Hayden!" Winnie screamed.

The elves looked up and over at Winnie,

anger burning in their eyes.

"Get behind us," Parker bravely stepped in front of Winnie.

Suddenly and without warning, the elves stopped and stood at attention before turning and running into the woods. Hayden lay on the ground, curled up in a ball.

"What just happened?" Sophie asked. "Where did they go?"

"Hayden," Winnie gasped, rushing to his side.

"Don't touch him," Max warned, just as Winnie reached out to her friend.

Hayden stayed in a ball as they all surrounded him. They could hear him sniffing.

Slowly, he pushed himself into a sitting position, tears running down his face.

Winnie desperately fought the urge to comfort him, reaching out her hand once again. Max had to grab her wrist, pulling her back while silently shaking his head no.

"What happened to them?" Hayden cried. "Why are they acting like this?"

"I don't know," Winnie said, the same questions running through her own mind.

"I'm scared," Hayden whimpered.

Pulling his knees to his chest, Hayden laid his head down onto his arms. His body shook as he cried. Violet felt her own eyes filling with tears, her heart breaking for the elves and the thought of Christmas being destroyed.

Kneeling next to him, Violet placed a hand on his arm. Hayden smiled as he looked up at her. Slowly, he moved his hand to cover hers.

"You can't save us," he hissed before breaking into a fit of laughter.

Violet pulled her hand out of his grip and stumbled back away from him, falling onto the ground.

Hayden's laughter became louder and more deranged. His clothes started to flash colors, turning from bright red to bright green and flashing through all the colors of the rainbow before fading to a dull grey. His hat faded from its bright blue to match the grey of his shirt and pants.

Hayden stood up and faced Winnie.

"You're next," he said in the robotic voice of the changed elves.

Hayden pointed his finger at Winnie before turning and dashing into the woods.

"We have to follow him," Parker yelled, running after him.

"Parker, wait," Max yelled, but she was already gone. "I'm going after her. You three stay here."

Scout appeared out of nowhere.

"I'll go with them," he said and took off after Max.

"Where did *he* come from?" Sophie asked, surprised by the elf's sudden appearance.

"He's always around," Winnie said. "Let's go wait in the barn."

Chapter Six

A Discovery in the Woods

Scout caught up to Max in less than a minute. They spotted Parker weaving through the trees a few feet in front of them.

Suddenly, Parker jumped behind a tree. She looked up and noticed Max and Scout in the woods behind her. She motioned for them to get down. They kept low as they ran to meet her.

"Hayden went in there," she whispered, pointing past the tree.

Max and Scout peeked around the tree. A single, small cottage sat in the middle of a clearing.

"I've never seen this place before," Scout commented. "And I've been everywhere in these woods."

"Look, there's a window," Parker pointed. "Let's go spy."

With a mysterious eyebrow wiggle, Parker crept quickly over to the side of the cottage, stopping directly under the window.

"Stay low," Scout said.

He stood up and peeked into the cottage. Curious, Parker stretched up just enough to see through the window, too.

Inside the cottage, a group of grey-clad elves gathered in a small room. They were standing in several lines, looking like statues, unmoving. Then, someone entered the room and made their way to the front.

"It's a human," Parker whispered. "A woman."

"Krystal!" Scout whispered anxiously.

"Look! A reindeer," Parker said.

Krystal was pulling a reindeer into the room behind her.

"It's Dancer," Scout confirmed.

Krystal was saying something, and all the elves started chanting again. Suddenly, a flash of light filled the small room, and Dancer was gone.

"Where did he go?" Parker asked.

Krystal bent down, picking something up.

When she stood up, she held a small figurine in her hand.

"Is that...?" Parker started.

"She just turned Dancer into a toy," Scout finished.

Krystal set the figurine on the mantel just as a few more elves appeared, pulling in another reindeer.

"Oh no, she has another one," Scout said. "We have to go, **now**!"

Without hesitation, the three ran back through the woods. They spotted the girls standing near the reindeer pen.

"Now, Vixen is missing," Winnie said as the three approached from the woods.

"They have her," Parker said between heavy breaths. "She's turned them into toys."

"What? Toys?" Winnie was horrified.

"We followed Hayden into the woods," Max explained. "We found a cottage, and all the elves were there."

"I've never seen that cottage before," Scout added. "Worse yet, it's Krystal who's controlling the elves!"

"Krystal is behind this?" Santa's voice boomed across the yard.

"Who is Krystal?" Sophie asked, looking from Scout to Winnie to Santa and back again.

"Krystal is my sister," Santa told her.

"You have a sister?" Violet was shocked.

"I do," Santa said sadly. "Or I did. I haven't seen her in many years, not since the night I…"

"Why don't I tell the story to the kids,"

Winnie offered, seeing the pain in Santa's eyes. "Scout can fill you in on everything else that's happened."

Santa gave a thankful nod as he followed Scout back toward the house.

"To start, you should know that Santa isn't the original Santa Claus," Winnie began. "His father was Santa and his father before him, and so on and so forth for hundreds of years."

The children nodded as Winnie continued.

"Krystal and Kris, as Santa was called when they were both younger, started out building toys together in the Workshop. When they were older, Krystal became Head Builder and ran the Workshop. Back then, Krystal was a lot of fun. She always came up with fun new toys, and she had all the elves laughing all day long.

"Krystal dreamed of more. She became bored with the Workshop and wanted to deliver the toys she had helped build. Kris knew how much she wanted to wear the Santa suit. Together, they made a pact that they would share the role of Santa when their time came. They would alternate years; first, Kris would deliver the toys, and the following year Krystal would get a chance.

"Together, they approached their father and shared their vision. He agreed it was a fantastic idea. Their father promised to create a second suit for Krystal since the suit holds the magic.

"When the time finally came, their father passed the suit down to Kris, and only Kris. He had not made a second suit for Krystal as promised."

"Wow, that's harsh," Sophie said.

"We all thought so," Winnie explained. "Krystal was pretty upset, which is understandable, but what she did next was unimaginable."

"What did she do?" Parker was captivated.

"She tried to destroy Christmas," Winnie told them flatly. "Their father later told Kris about the greed he had seen in Krystal and feared she would want too much power. He feared that her greed would eventually destroy Christmas for all time.

"It turns out their father was right. That year, Krystal almost destroyed Christmas. She went on a rampage in the Workshop, destroying everything in her path. All the toys we had worked all year to create were demolished in a matter of minutes. Several elves tried to stop her, but she shoved and pushed them out of her way, injuring many of them.

"Santa was very angry; I've never seen him that angry," Winnie shivered at the memory. "He was mostly angry because elves were hurt. Krystal took her anger out on all the children of the world by trying to destroy Christmas. Santa was devastated because his father had been right; her anger showed she couldn't be trusted to ever wear the suit. So, he banished her."

"Wow," Violet said, her eyes wide. "That's intense."

"It took everything we had to save Christmas," Winnie told them. "Elves and

Santa worked around the clock. We didn't eat or sleep for days at a time; it was the roughest few weeks in our lives. Somehow, we managed to fix everything, and Christmas was saved."

"Help!" Scout came rushing toward them, out of breath, and panicked, breaking everyone from the story. "They took Santa!"

Chapter Seven

Captured

"We have to get back to the cottage," Parker said, knowing without a shred of doubt *that* is where the elves would take Santa.

"Follow me," Scout shouted as he headed back into the woods.

The children and Winnie followed Scout, hoping they wouldn't be too late.

"The cottage is straight ahead," Scout told them, slowing down and pointing. "We have to stay low and stay quiet."

They crept toward the cottage and knelt under the window. Cautiously, Scout peered through the window, and the rest followed, their eyes barely above the windowsill.

The elves were gathered in the small room. This time they stood in a circle, surrounding Santa, who sat tied up in the middle of the floor, his mouth covered. A loud cackle filled the air as Krystal walked in.

Krystal pushed through the elves, making her way toward the center of the circle.

Parker carefully pushed on the window, surprised by how easily it opened. Silently warning the others to be quiet, she shoved the window open a bit wider to hear what was happening inside.

"Well, well, if it isn't my dear brother,"

Krystal said, her voice dripping with disgust. "Finally, I can take back the suit you stole from me."

Santa made muffled noises and struggled against the ropes holding him in place.

"Oh, the disappointed looks on the faces of all those children when they find nothing under the tree on Christmas morning," she taunted. "Or maybe I'll find a way to send the broken toys; that will teach those brats! Kids everywhere, crying. It will be music to my ears."

Santa was shaking his head furiously, his eyes wide.

"I can see the headlines now, 'Santa destroys Christmas for all the boys and girls,'" Krystal taunted. "Everyone will hate you, and Christmas will be no more."

Santa looked up at Krystal, sadness filling his eyes.

"Do you have something to say, Dear Brother?" Krystal asked, ripping the gag from his mouth.

"Why are you doing this?" Santa gasped.

"Oh, Kris," Krystal said. "*You* made a promise to me, and *you* broke it. Then you banished me."

"You hurt the elves," Santa protested.

"You hurt me!" Krystal spat out. "You turned your back on me, just like our father did."

"Krystal..."

"Enough!" she yelled, and with a snap of her fingers, Santa was gone.

Outside, the kids gasped in shock.

Krystal was laughing again as she bent

down to pick up the toy she had just created. With a satisfied smile, she set the toy Santa next to the two tiny reindeer on the mantle.

"Bring me the rest of the reindeer," Krystal ordered the elves.

The elves immediately began to pour out of the room.

"Get behind the house, quick!" Scout said, jumping back from the window. "Don't let them see us."

They managed to duck behind the side of the cottage seconds before the elves ran out.

"That was close," Sophie said breathlessly.

Parker had gone back to the window and was looking inside.

"What are you doing?" Sophie hissed, still hiding behind the cottage.

"It's empty," Parker replied.

Parker quickly climbed through the open window and crept quietly toward the mantle. Grabbing the figures, she hurried back out the window. Noticing the glare from her oldest sister, Parker opened her hand. Everyone looked down at the toys in Parker's palm.

Suddenly, Winnie's head snapped up, her eyes grew wide with fear.

"Oh no, we have to get back to the reindeer!" she cried. "The elves are on their way to capture them now. We have to stop them."

They all ran as fast as they could back toward the barn. From the safety of the trees, they could see several elves surrounding the pen; the reindeer huddled together in the middle, looking frightened.

"We need a plan," Max told them urgently.

"Good idea," Sophie agreed. "What's the plan?"

"I don't know," he shrugged. "I don't have one. I just know we need one. We can't just run in there; there are too many of them."

"If we can figure out how to turn the elves back, we can all go after Krystal," Violet looked deep in thought.

"How are we supposed to do that?" Sophie asked.

"Figure out what changed them in the first place," Max said as if it were that simple. "Then, reverse it."

"Maybe it works like a virus," Violet said. "The elves changed only after they were touched by a grey elf, right? That's why you two are still fine because you haven't been touched."

"So, we need a vaccine?" Sophie asked, thinking back to science class.

"That would be helpful," Violet commented.

"We need to find patient zero," Max informed them.

"Patient zero?" Winnie asked. "What is that?"

"More like *who* is that?" Max answered. "Patient zero refers to the first person who gets infected. They are responsible for passing a virus on."

"That's it, then," Violet chimed in. "We need to figure out who the first elf to change was."

The children all turned to look at Winnie

and Scout.

"It happened so fast," Winnie said. "One day, only a few elves were acting up, and by the end of the week, most elves had changed."

"Can you remember who turned grey first?" Sophie asked.

"Let's see," Winnie tried to remember. "Last week, Ginger and Spice were in the Workshop ripping up dolls. Now, that I think about it, their hats weren't as brightly colored as normal."

"It was around that time we first started to link the grey outfits to the bad elves," Scout added. His eyes lit up. "Wait, I remember seeing Harper sneaking out of the kitchen with a plate of cookies. She was in a hurry, and she was taking them into the woods!"

"Was she grey?" Sophie asked.

"I remember thinking at the time, she was wearing the wrong hat," Scout told them. "Now it all makes sense; her hat was grey!"

"Harper works in the Workshop," Winnie added. "Right next to Ginger and Spice!"

"Harper is patient zero!" Scout exclaimed, giving Winnie a high five.

"Let's go find her," Parker said.

Chapter Eight

The Plan

"Not so fast," Max stepped in front of Parker before she could run off. "We know Harper is patient zero, but how do we break the spell?"

"It all began with Harper," Violet said. "If we can change her, maybe it would cause a chain reaction that turns all the elves back."

"That sounds ridiculous," Sophie sighed.

"Look around you, Sophie," Max said. "I

once thought this whole place was a ridiculous idea, yet here we are."

"Fine. Let's say your idea actually works," Sophie said. "How do we change her?"

All eyes turned to Violet, who immediately felt uncomfortable. She shrugged and stared at the ground.

"You've gotten us this far in the plan, Violet," Max encouraged. "What do you think?"

"Okay," Violet said quietly, thinking. "Right before the elves changed, they were crying."

"They were laughing like crazed monkeys, actually," Parker pointed out.

"True, but before the laughing, they were crying," Violet repeated.

Everyone nodded in agreement, brows

furrowed in deep thought.

"Maybe we need to make them happy," Violet suggested. "Maybe sadness is the trigger that brings on the change."

"How do we make an elf happy?" Parker asked.

All eyes turned back to Winnie and Scout.

"Making toys," Scout began to list off his favorite things. "Laughing with each other, friendship, hot chocolate, and cookies."

"Christmas," Winnie blurted out. "We spend all year preparing for Christmas. We want it to be a magical experience for all the children of the world."

"That's it," Violet shouted. "Christmas is so much more than toys and Santa; it's all about the children. Children are what make elves happy."

"That's true," Winnie agreed. "It's all about making children happy."

"That's why we're here," Violet continued. "We're here to save the elves because *we're* the only ones who can."

"That makes perfect sense," Max's eyes lit with surprise.

Violet gave a shy smile.

"I'll go find Harper," Scout told them.

They watched in amazement as he darted in and out of the barn, undetected. He returned to the group, out of breath but excited.

"I found her," Scout said. "She's in the barn trying to trap Blitzen, but she's not alone. Ginger and Spice are with her."

They followed Scout down to the barn and stood outside the door, peering in.

"We still need a plan," Max whispered.

"Where are the exits?" Parker asked, taking charge.

"This door," Scout put his hand on the door where they were currently standing. "Each stall has a door that leads outside, but it looks like the elves closed those already."

"Do you have some rope?" Parker asked.

"Loads," Scout pointed into the barn where several lines of rope hung along the wall.

"Okay, here's the plan," Parker started. "Each kid will grab a rope. Then, we go into the stall, grab the elves, and tie them up. Winnie and Scout, you stand guard at this door. Once everything is secure, we make Harper laugh and the spell will be broken."

"Make sure you both stay out of the way,"

Max reminded Winnie and Scout.

"Ready?" Parker asked.

Everyone nodded in agreement, and Parker led the way into the barn. Winnie made sure to shut and lock the door behind them.

Each kid grabbed some rope and tiptoed toward the stall door. Parker held up her hand and counted to five. On five, she shoved the stall door open. The three grey elves stopped what they were doing and looked blankly at the children.

"Grab an elf," Parker shouted.

Max and Sophie went after Ginger and Spice, tackling them to the ground and holding tight. Parker jumped on Harper.

"Violet, you have to tie them up," Parker yelled towards Violet. "We can't hold the elves and tie them at the same time!"

Violet fumbled with her rope, dropping it while she desperately searched for the end.

"Hurry," Max yelled.

"I'm trying," Violet yelled back in frustration.

Scout was at her side instantly, finding the end of the rope and running toward Parker. Quickly, he wound the rope around the struggling grey elf, careful to avoid her touch.

"Put them back-to-back," Violet yelled.

Max and Sophie held the elves in place, while Violet quickly wrapped a rope around them. Sophie took over tying the knots while Max rushed over to help secure Harper.

"Now what?" Sophie asked Violet.

"Let's...make her happy?" Violet guessed.

"Destroy Christmas," Harper growled mechanically, struggling against the ropes holding her.

"You love Christmas," Violet reminded her. "Try to remember, Harper. The trees decorated with lights and ornaments, singing carols, spending time with family and friends. Happiness and laughter shared around a table full of delicious foods."

"Eating so much, your tummy feels like it will explode," Parker added, her mouth watering at the thought.

"Brightly wrapped presents under the tree," Sophie said.

"Staying up late waiting for Santa," said Parker.

"Spreading joy and cheer across the world," Violet added. "One silent night full of anticipation as kids everywhere fight sleep."

"Happy, excited kids," Max chimed in. "That's what you do, Harper. You bring happiness to children like me."

"And me," Parker said.

"And me," Sophie agreed.

"It's our job, Harper," Winnie reminded her. "It's what we get up every morning for; to bring happiness to all the children."

Harper began to glow.

"Something is happening," Violet whispered in amazement.

A smile began to form across Harper's face. Memories of Christmas flooded her mind.

Slowly, color began to creep back into her clothes, starting at her feet and moving all the way up until her hat was teal blue once again. She blinked a few times and then looked at the children smiling in front of her.

"Wh..what happened?" Harper asked, noticing the ropes holding her.

"It worked," Winnie said.

Winnie untied Harper while quickly explaining what had happened. Harper walked over to Ginger and Spice and lightly tapped each one on the shoulder. They, too, began to glow, and soon color had returned to their clothes.

"Now I play tag," Harper laughed.

"Not so fast!" Krystal's voice boomed through the barn.

Chapter Nine

Saving Christmas

"It's over," Max said bravely. "Your spell is broken."

"The elves may be free, but their destruction remains," Krystal laughed. "You'll never save Christmas in time. Besides, Santa is a useless toy right now. I'll change all the reindeer into toys as well."

"You'll never get to them," Parker stood next to her brother.

"Are you going to stop me?" Krystal laughed down at them. "I'll turn every last one of you into toys!"

Krystal raised her hand and aimed at Parker. Parker squeezed her eyes shut, bracing for impact. She felt a shove and her body hit the ground.

Parker, expecting to be a toy, opened her eyes, surprised to realize she was fine. Glancing up, she looked toward her brother and sisters, who were staring at her.

No, they weren't staring at *her*; they were staring at something *next* to her.

"Scout!" Parker yelled.

Scout was lying on the ground beside her. He had been turned into a toy.

Parker pushed herself up and ran full steam at Krystal, slamming her shoulder into

Krystal's stomach. They both fell to the ground, Parker landing on top of Krystal.

"You brat," Krystal yelled, shoving Parker off her. "This time, I won't miss."

"No!" Max yelled, running toward Krystal, who was still on the ground.

Protection mode kicking in, Violet and Sophie joined in the fight. The children piled onto Krystal, struggling to hold her down.

"I've got some rope," Winnie yelled.

Winnie, Ginger, and Spice helped the children wrap the rope securely around Krystal. Everyone stepped back, exhausted and breathless.

"I'll go free the elves," Harper said, rushing out of the barn.

"It's over," Max told Krystal once again.

Krystal began to laugh.

"It will never be over."

Krystal snapped her fingers. With a flash of light, she disappeared, the ropes left lying in a heap.

"Where did she go?" Sophie looked around.

"She's gone," Winnie said quietly. "Hopefully, she won't come back anytime soon."

"We have a lot of clean-up to do," Ginger commented, looking around the barn.

"You have no idea," Winnie said. "The cursed elves caused a lot of damage."

"We'll start organizing all the elves," Spice offered. "As soon as they change back, we'll get everyone to work."

Ginger and Spice left the barn, rounding up the elves and quickly explaining what had happened as best they could.

"What about Santa?" Parker asked sadly, pulling the toy figurines out of her pocket. "How do we change them all back?"

Parker gently placed Santa and the two reindeer figures next to the toy Scout. Everyone stared down at the tiny toys.

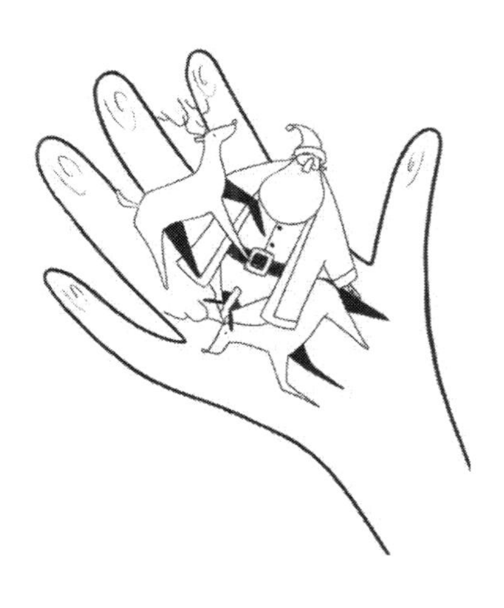

"After all we did, we couldn't save them," Violet said, picking up the Scout toy and holding him in her palm. "That's so unfair."

A single tear ran down her cheek, falling directly onto the toy figure of Scout. The toy lifted out of her hand and into the air. Slowly, it began spinning around several times until Scout stood, full-sized, in front of them.

"Scout!" Violet threw her arms around the elf.

"What happened?" Scout asked. "I feel a little dizzy."

"She turned you into a toy," Winnie told him.

"Tears of a child," Parker said, shaking her head and sounding like a grown-up.

The siblings all looked at her and laughed.

"Can you bring the rest back?" Winnie

asked.

"I still have some tears left," Violet said.

Violet leaned down in front of Santa and the two reindeer, closing her eyes. The tears that had been brimming on the surface fell onto the figures. The toys lifted into the air and spun around until Santa, Dancer, and Vixen stood in front of them, looking dazed and confused.

"Where is Krystal?" Santa growled.

"She vanished," Winnie told him. "Disappeared into thin air."

"I'm sure we haven't heard the last from her," Santa let out a big sigh. He turned toward the children. "You kids did it. You saved the elves, and you saved me. You saved Christmas!"

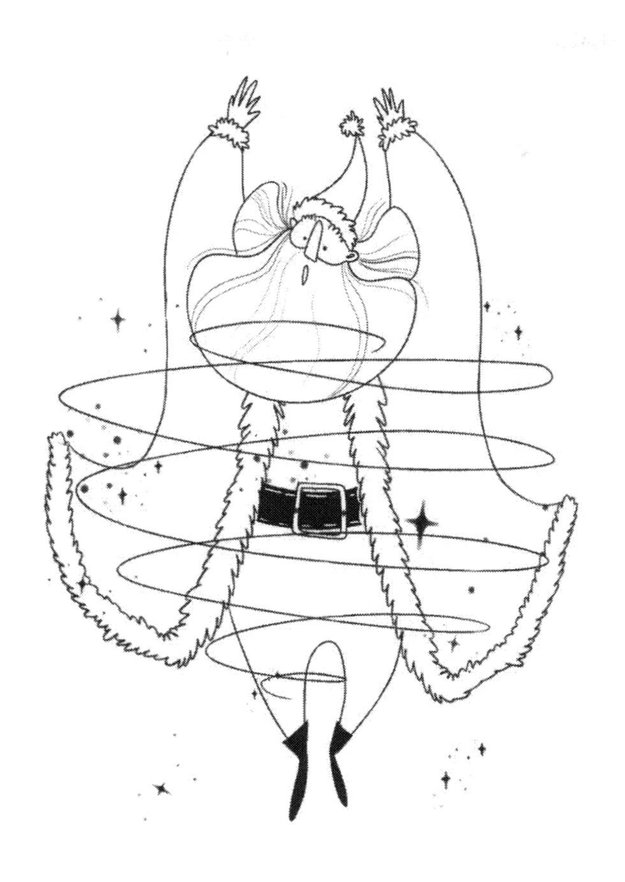

"The elves are starting the clean-up," Winnie told him. "We should be able to get back on schedule in no time, thanks to the children."

"We can help with the clean-up," Max offered.

"You've done enough for us here," Santa said. "I think it's time for you to get back home."

"Mom and Dad must be so worried," Sophie said, concerned.

"They're probably angry, too," Max commented.

"We'll be grounded for sure," Parker moaned.

"I'm sure you'll be just fine," Santa laughed. "Thank you for all you did here today. Scout, take them home."

Santa turned toward the Workshop as Winnie wiped at her eyes.

"Thank you so much," she said. "Sorry, I'm getting all emotional. It's just, you brought my friends back, and you saved Christmas."

Winnie wrapped them all in a hug for several seconds. She waved goodbye as Scout led them back into the forest.

"This will get you home," Scout handed Max the magic cube.

Max took the cube, pushing the buttons and pulling on the lever.

"Thanks for choosing us, Scout," he said, sliding the magic cube into his pocket.

"The *cube* choose you," Scout replied with a wink. "Merry Christmas."

"You too," Sophie turned to give Scout

one last hug, but he was gone.

"Let's go home," Max said.

The four children walked *into* the trees and found themselves walking *out* of the shed.

"We're back," Parker said.

"How are we going to explain this to Mom and Dad?" Sophie asked nervously.

With their heads down, they walked into the kitchen, the air smelling of pancakes.

"I'm starving," Parker suddenly realized they hadn't eaten for a long time.

"Good thing, because breakfast is ready," Mom called out. "Go wash up so we can eat."

The children walked through the kitchen, exchanging startled glances. Mom was setting the table while Dad sat still reading his book.

"What are you gawking at?" their dad

asked.

"Nothing," Max said quickly, leading the way down to the washroom.

"It's like we've only been gone for a few minutes," Sophie commented once they were out of earshot.

"That's so cool," Parker said.

"Do you think we'll ever go back?" Violet asked.

Max reached in his pocket to grab the magic cube, but it was no longer there.

"I hope so," he commented.

The End

Thank you for taking the time to read *"The Mystery of the Cursed Evles."* I hope you enjoyed the story.

I love writing the Magic Cube Adventures and would love to share these books with readers everywhere. As a self-published author, reviews are the best way to show others how much you enjoyed a book. If you liked this book, it would be fantastic if you would give it a rating on Amazon and/or GoodReads. If you leave a short review, that would be helpful as well.

https://www.amazon.com/Mystery-Cursed-Elves-Magic-Cube-ebook/dp/B08HJR1W3C

Writing a Simple Review:

Pick one or all options below:

A) What was your favorite part of the story?
B) Who were your favorite characters and why?
C) Would you recommend this

Curious where the Magic Cube came from? Join our mailing list to receive exclusive content, including a free, six-chapter Prequel story, the first look at illustrations, cover reveals, chapter excerpts, book recommendations, and more.

www.mitchelmareee.com

Don't miss the next exciting book in the Magic Cube Series:

Sophie began wiggling and squirming. "My back itches."

"Mine too," Parker said, giving up on climbing the rocks. Instead, she leaned her back against it and moved up and down as if it were a scratching post.

"It's so itchy," Sophie wiggled around, stretching one arm behind her but unable to reach the itch. "Scratch it! Scratch it!" She turned her back towards Violet, begging for help.

"It's tickling me," Parker laughed as she squirmed about. "Is there something crawling on me?"

Violet reached out to scratch at Sophie's

back but stopped short when they heard a tearing sound.

"Did my shirt just rip?" Sophie strained her neck, trying to see.

"Ahhh!" Violet yelled, jumping back, and pointing. "What is that?"

"What? Is it a bug?" Sophie screeched, shaking herself and jumping up and down. "Get it off! Get it off!"

Max jumped down from the rocks and rushed over to Sophie, curious to learn what the yelling was about. Sure enough, Sophie's shirt had two rips over both shoulder blades. Two blue specks poked out of the newly made holes. As if attached to a spring, two bright blue wings popped out of Sophie's back. Max managed to jump back just in time to avoid being smacked in the face.

At that exact moment, Parker heard her shirt rip. "What the heck? This shirt is brand new. Mom is going to freak."

Parker's concern was quickly forgotten when two purple wings sprang out through each tear. She whipped her head from side to side, examining the wings. "Whoa! Cool!"

"Wings!" Violet yelled, looking from one set of wings to the other. "You both have wings!"

Acknowledgments

This book would not be possible without the help, inspiration, and encouragement of my husband, Kevin. Thank you for believing in me.

Thank you to my children. This is as much your book as it is mine. Thank you for your ideas and your imaginations.

Thank you to my parents for always believing I had a story to tell.

Thank you to my grandmother for introducing me to the joy of reading and always encouraging me to write.

Thank you to Wes Mills for helping to make the story better.

Thank you to Darcy Jayne for correcting all my mistakes and enhancing the final copy.

Thank you to Ola Snimshchikova for bringing the story alive with your illustrations.

A huge thank you to all my Kickstarter

backers without you, this book would not be possible: Corei Bean; Kari and Thomas Bosley; Adam Hitchcock; Brenda Kelso, Julian Kelso, and Izaak King II; Brad, Theresa, and Bryce Alford; Wendy and Bruce Peterson; David "Fish Fillet" Blackwell; Ryan, Shelly, Emily, and Grace La Vergne; Jim Terryberry; Team PhillFam; Michael and Vanessa Patrick; Sean Byrne; Sean Robbins; Kara VanWinkle; Emree Reesman; Mikey Jensen; Jessica and Zach Peterson; Darcy Jayne; Eunice Hammerstrom; Brian and Lisa Peterson; Samantha Nixon; Lanette and Amber Allen; Justin and Marti Thomas; and all the backers who wish to remain anonymous.

About the Author

Mitchel Maree writes children's fantasy and adventure fiction. Her inspiration comes from days spent with her children talking of unicorns, elves, fairies, dragons, giants, and all things magical.

Mitchel Maree currently resides in Dublin, Ireland, with her husband and children.